Published by Doubleday, a division of
Bantam Doubleday Dell Publishing Group, Inc.,
666 Fifth Avenue, New York, New York 10103

Doubleday and the portrayal of an anchor with a dolphin
are trademarks of Doubleday,
a division of Bantam Doubleday Dell Publishing Group, Inc.

Library of Congress Cataloging-in-Publication Data
Darke, Alison Claire.
The nightingale / by Hans Christian Andersen; illustrated by
Alison Claire Darke.—1st ed.   p. cm.
Summary: Though the Emperor neglects the nightingale in preference
for a jeweled mechanical imitation, the little bird returns to
revive the dying ruler with its beautiful song.
[1. Fairy tales. 2. Nightingales—Fiction.]   I. Andersen, H. C.
(Hans Christian), 1805-1875. Nattergalen.   II. Title.
PZ8.D189Ni 1989   839.8′ 136—dc19   [E]   88-28234   CIP   AC
ISBN 0-385-26081-4 (Trade)   ISBN 0-385-26082-2 (Library)   RL: 3.6

Printed in Belgium by Proost
First Edition in the United States of America, 1989
1089

THE NIGHTINGALE

HANS CHRISTIAN ANDERSEN
ILLUSTRATED BY ALISON CLAIRE DARKE

DOUBLEDAY
NEW YORK LONDON TORONTO SYDNEY AUCKLAND

Long ago in China there lived a very rich and powerful Emperor. His palace was the most magnificent in the world. It was made of fine porcelain, priceless but so fragile that you had to watch your step in case you broke something. In the garden were the most wonderful flowers. The most splendid of all had little silver bells tied to them and they tinkled so that no one could pass by without noticing them.

The garden was so big that even the gardener didn't know where it ended. If you went on walking, you reached a lovely forest with tall trees and deep lakes. The forest went right down to the blue sea, where great ships could sail in under the branches of the trees.

And in the forest lived a nightingale, who sang so beautifully that even the poor hardworking fisherman would stop casting his nets every night and listen to its song.

"Lord, how beautiful it is," he would say.

From all corners of the world travelers came and marveled at the Emperor's city and the palace and the garden too. But when they heard the nightingale they said, "This is more wonderful than all the rest."

The travelers talked about it when they got home, and scholars wrote many books about the city, the palace and the garden, but they always ended by saying that the most beautiful thing was the song of the nightingale.

These books went round the world and one day some of them reached the Emperor. He sat in his golden chair and read and read, nodding his head with pleasure at the splendid descriptions of the city, the palace and the garden. Then he came to: "But the nightingale is the best of all."

"What's this?" said the Emperor. "The nightingale? I know nothing of it. Is there such a bird in my empire — and in my own garden?"

He called for his grand lord-in-waiting.

"They say there's a most remarkable bird here called a nightingale," said the Emperor. "It's said to be the finest thing throughout my great empire. Why have I never been told about it?"

"I've never heard of it," said the lord-in-waiting. "It's never been presented at court."

"It's my wish it should come here this evening and sing for me," commanded the Emperor. "It's a fine thing when the whole world knows what I have, except me."

"I've never heard of it," repeated the lord-in-waiting. "But I shall find it."

The lord-in-waiting ran up and down all the stairs, through halls and corridors, but nobody he met had ever heard of the nightingale. He ran back again to the Emperor and said it must be a tale made up by those who wrote books.

"But the book I read it in," said the Emperor, "was sent to me by the high and mighty Emperor of Japan, so it must be true. I will hear the nightingale. It must be here this evening."

"Tsing-pe!" said the lord-in-waiting and ran once more up and down the stairs and through all the halls and corridors. Half the court ran with him, anxious to carry out the Emperor's command, and asking after this remarkable nightingale that the whole world knew about
— but no one at court had ever heard of.

At last they found a little girl in the kitchen.

She said, "Oh goodness yes, the nightingale. Of course I know it. Every evening they let me take a few leftovers to my mother. She lives down by the seashore, so when I'm on my way back and feel tired, I take a rest in the woods and hear the nightingale sing. It makes tears come into my eyes, just like Mother kissing me."

"My dear little kitchen-maid," said the lord-in-waiting, "I'll get you a permanent appointment in the kitchen and permission to see the Emperor eating, if only you can take us to the nightingale. Its presence is commanded by the Emperor for this evening."

So they all made their way into the forest where the nightingale usually sang. As they were going along, a cow began to moo.

"Oh," said the court page, "now we've found it. What a powerful voice for such a small creature. I'm quite certain I've heard it before."

"No, that's a cow mooing," said the kitchen-maid. "We're still a long way from the nightingale's home."

The frogs were croaking in the pond.

"Lovely," said the Master of the Imperial Household.

"Now I can hear the song — it's just like tiny church bells."

"No, that's the frogs," said the little kitchen-maid.

And then the nightingale began to sing.

"That's it," said the little girl. "Look, it's sitting up there." And she pointed to a little gray bird up in the branches.

"Is that it?" said the lord-in-waiting. "How ordinary it looks. It's undoubtedly lost its color at seeing so many grand people."

"Little nightingale," called the kitchen-maid, "our gracious Emperor wishes you to sing for him."

"With the greatest of pleasure," said the nightingale, and sang so beautifully it was a joy to hear.

"It's just like glass bells!" said the lord-in-waiting. "And look at the way its little throat quivers. It's remarkable we've never heard it before."

"Shall I sing again for the Emperor?" asked the nightingale, thinking the Emperor was there.

"My excellent little nightingale," said the lord-in-waiting, "I have great pleasure in inviting you this evening to a celebration at court, where you will charm His Imperial Grace with your enchanting song."

"It sounds best outside in the forest," said the nightingale but, as it was the Emperor's wish, it came with them quite happily.

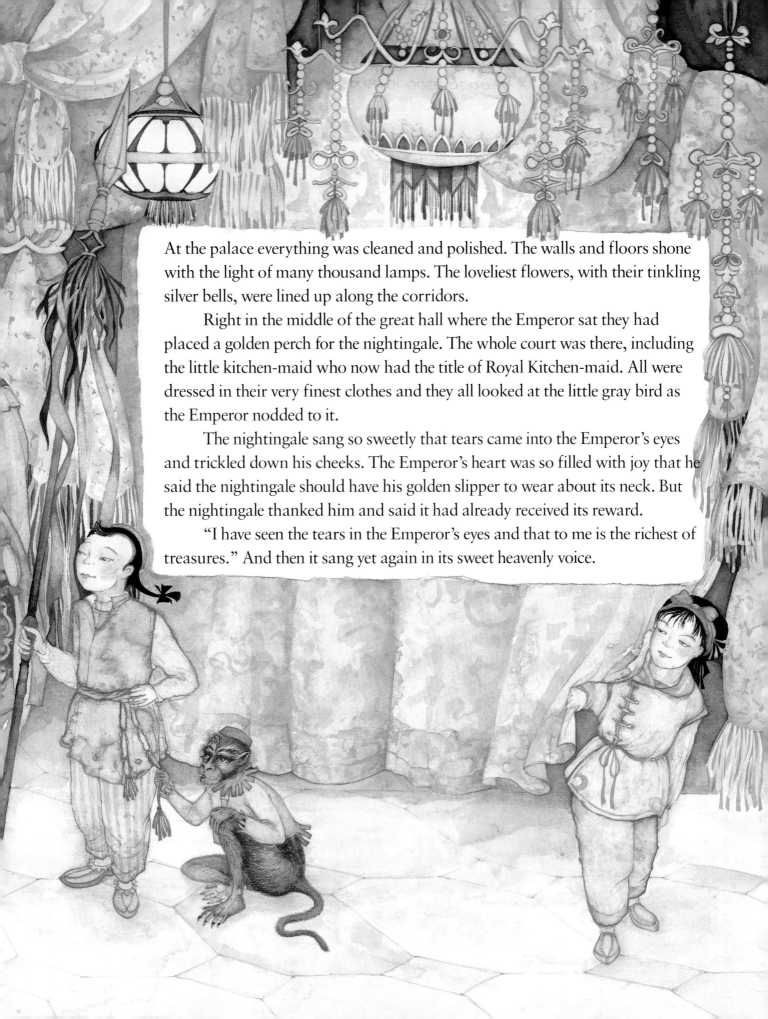

At the palace everything was cleaned and polished. The walls and floors shone with the light of many thousand lamps. The loveliest flowers, with their tinkling silver bells, were lined up along the corridors.

Right in the middle of the great hall where the Emperor sat they had placed a golden perch for the nightingale. The whole court was there, including the little kitchen-maid who now had the title of Royal Kitchen-maid. All were dressed in their very finest clothes and they all looked at the little gray bird as the Emperor nodded to it.

The nightingale sang so sweetly that tears came into the Emperor's eyes and trickled down his cheeks. The Emperor's heart was so filled with joy that he said the nightingale should have his golden slipper to wear about its neck. But the nightingale thanked him and said it had already received its reward.

"I have seen the tears in the Emperor's eyes and that to me is the richest of treasures." And then it sang yet again in its sweet heavenly voice.

The Emperor decreed that the nightingale was now to remain at court, where it was to have its own cage. It was free to fly outside twice during the day and twice during the night. Twelve servants were to go with it, each holding fast to a silken ribbon tied round the bird's leg. There was, of course, no pleasure for the nightingale in going out like that.

One day a large parcel came for the Emperor. On the outside was written: NIGHTINGALE.

"We've a new book here about our famous bird," said the Emperor.

But it wasn't a book; it was a clockwork nightingale, made to look like the real one, but studded all over with diamonds and rubies and sapphires. As soon as it was wound up, it sang one of the real nightingale's songs. Its tail, glittering with silver and gold, went up and down in time with the music. Round its neck was hung a little ribbon on which was written: THE EMPEROR OF JAPAN'S NIGHTINGALE IS A POOR THING COMPARED WITH THE EMPEROR OF CHINA'S.

"It's lovely," they all cried. "Now the birds can sing together — what a duet that'll be!"

And so the birds had to sing together, but it didn't sound right, for the real nightingale sang in its own way and the mechanical bird in clockwork time.

So then they made the clockwork bird sing by itself; it was just as great a success as the real one, and it was so very much more pleasing to look at, with its jewels glittering and sparkling.

Three and thirty times it sang the same piece, and it was not in the least bit tired. The court would willingly have heard it through again, but the Emperor thought the real nightingale should sing a little too. But where had it gone? It had flown out of the open window away to its green forest, and no one had noticed.

"What on earth can be the matter?" said the Emperor.

The courtiers tut-tutted and declared that it was an extremely ungrateful creature.

The Master of Music lavishly praised the clockwork bird, saying it was better than the real nightingale.

"For you see, my lords — and above all, Your Majesty — with the real nightingale you never know what's going to come next, but with the clockwork bird you can be absolutely certain."

"That's exactly what I think," they all said, and the Master of Music was given permission to show it to the people.

"They must hear it sing too," said the Emperor.

And hear it they did. They were all as pleased as if they had got merrily drunk on tea.

But the poor fisherman, who had heard the real nightingale, said, "It sounds pretty enough, quite like the real bird, but something's missing."

The real nightingale was banished from the Emperor's kingdom. The clockwork bird was kept on a silken cushion close by the Emperor's bed and it was given the rank of Singer-in-chief to the Imperial Bedside Table.

So it went on for a whole year. The Emperor, the court and all the people knew every little trill in the clockwork bird's song off by heart and they could now sing with it. The street urchins sang, "Ti-ti-tee, trill-trill-tri-i-ll!" and the Emperor sang as well. How wonderful it all was.

But one evening, when the clockwork bird was singing its best and the Emperor was lying in bed listening to it, something went "ping" inside the bird. Then, "whirr-r-r!" The wheels all whizzed round and the music stopped.

The Emperor leaped
out of bed and called for his
doctor, but what could he do?
So they sent for the clockmaker and, after much prodding and poking, he
got the bird to go again. But he said it must be used very sparingly because the
pins were badly worn and it was impossible to replace them without upsetting
the music. It was a great blow.

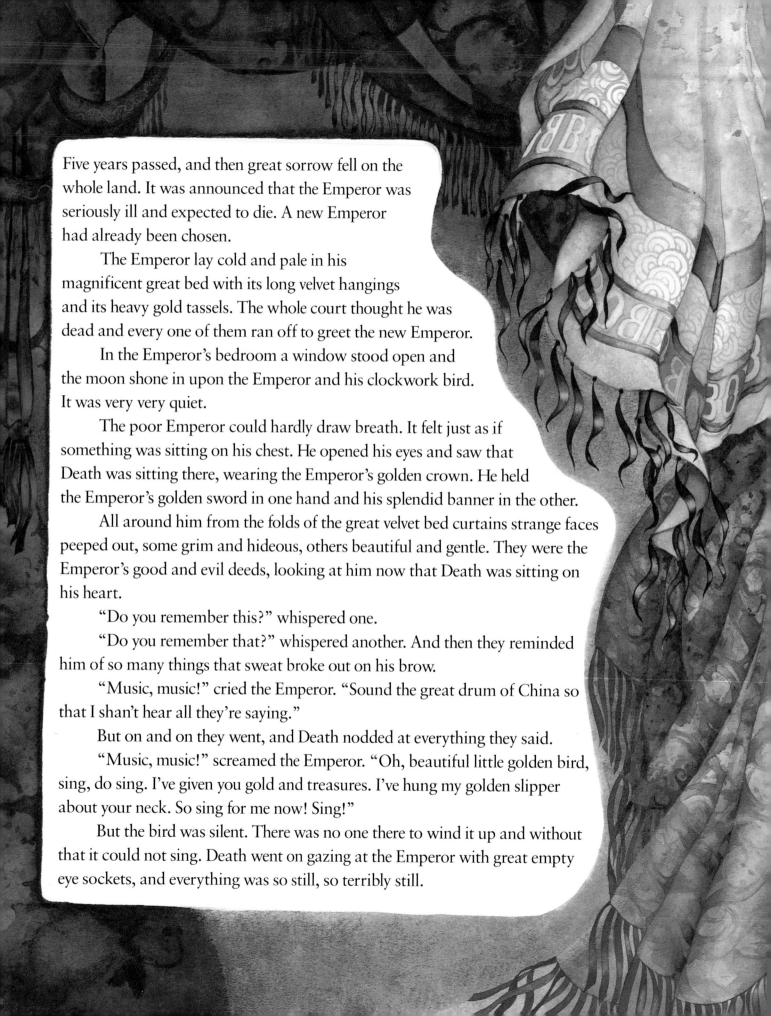

Five years passed, and then great sorrow fell on the whole land. It was announced that the Emperor was seriously ill and expected to die. A new Emperor had already been chosen.

The Emperor lay cold and pale in his magnificent great bed with its long velvet hangings and its heavy gold tassels. The whole court thought he was dead and every one of them ran off to greet the new Emperor.

In the Emperor's bedroom a window stood open and the moon shone in upon the Emperor and his clockwork bird. It was very very quiet.

The poor Emperor could hardly draw breath. It felt just as if something was sitting on his chest. He opened his eyes and saw that Death was sitting there, wearing the Emperor's golden crown. He held the Emperor's golden sword in one hand and his splendid banner in the other.

All around him from the folds of the great velvet bed curtains strange faces peeped out, some grim and hideous, others beautiful and gentle. They were the Emperor's good and evil deeds, looking at him now that Death was sitting on his heart.

"Do you remember this?" whispered one.

"Do you remember that?" whispered another. And then they reminded him of so many things that sweat broke out on his brow.

"Music, music!" cried the Emperor. "Sound the great drum of China so that I shan't hear all they're saying."

But on and on they went, and Death nodded at everything they said.

"Music, music!" screamed the Emperor. "Oh, beautiful little golden bird, sing, do sing. I've given you gold and treasures. I've hung my golden slipper about your neck. So sing for me now! Sing!"

But the bird was silent. There was no one there to wind it up and without that it could not sing. Death went on gazing at the Emperor with great empty eye sockets, and everything was so still, so terribly still.

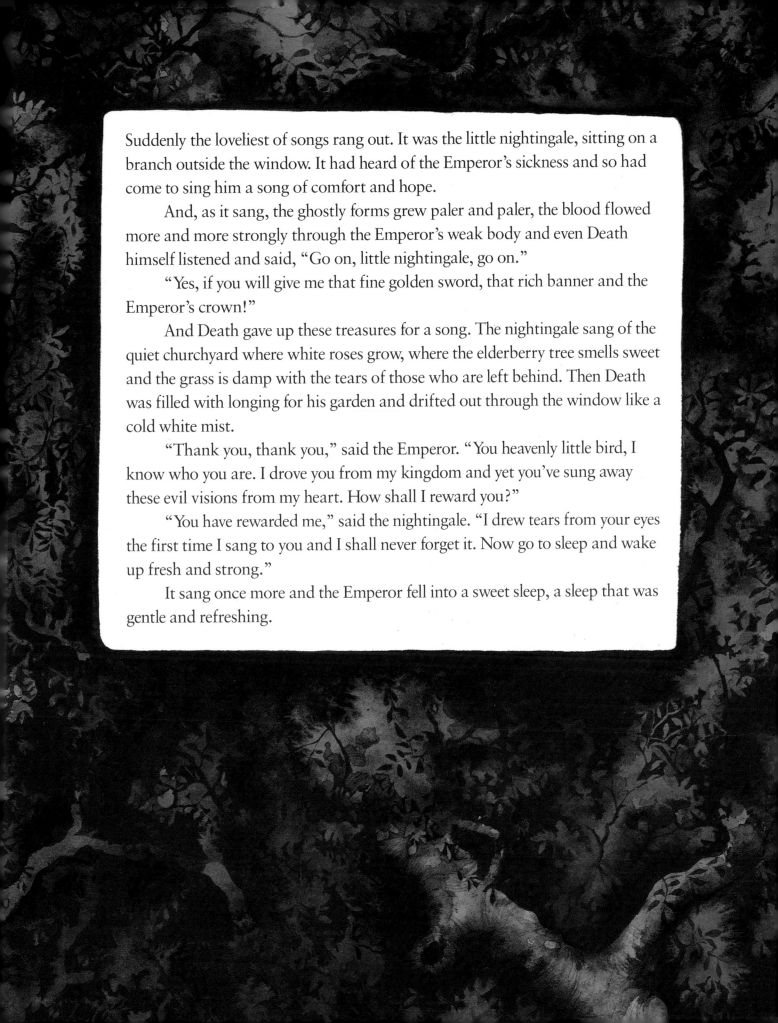

Suddenly the loveliest of songs rang out. It was the little nightingale, sitting on a branch outside the window. It had heard of the Emperor's sickness and so had come to sing him a song of comfort and hope.

And, as it sang, the ghostly forms grew paler and paler, the blood flowed more and more strongly through the Emperor's weak body and even Death himself listened and said, "Go on, little nightingale, go on."

"Yes, if you will give me that fine golden sword, that rich banner and the Emperor's crown!"

And Death gave up these treasures for a song. The nightingale sang of the quiet churchyard where white roses grow, where the elderberry tree smells sweet and the grass is damp with the tears of those who are left behind. Then Death was filled with longing for his garden and drifted out through the window like a cold white mist.

"Thank you, thank you," said the Emperor. "You heavenly little bird, I know who you are. I drove you from my kingdom and yet you've sung away these evil visions from my heart. How shall I reward you?"

"You have rewarded me," said the nightingale. "I drew tears from your eyes the first time I sang to you and I shall never forget it. Now go to sleep and wake up fresh and strong."

It sang once more and the Emperor fell into a sweet sleep, a sleep that was gentle and refreshing.

The sun was shining through the window when the Emperor woke up feeling strong and healthy again. None of his servants had returned, but the nightingale was still singing.

"You must stay with me forever," said the Emperor. "You shall sing only when you want to, and I'll break the clockwork bird into a thousand pieces."

"No, don't do that," said the nightingale. "It's done its best for you, so keep it. I cannot make my nest in your palace, but if you'll let me come when I wish, I'll sit on the branch by your window and sing for you. I shall sing about your kingdom and the people so you will know all that is going on. But one thing you must promise me."

"Anything," said the Emperor, standing there in his imperial robes again, holding the heavy gold sword to his heart.

"Tell no one about the little bird that tells you everything. It will be better for me if you don't." And then the nightingale flew away.

"I promise, my loyal little friend," the Emperor called after him. The servants came in to look upon their dead Emperor, and stood there, amazed.

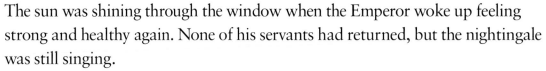

"Good morning!" said the Emperor.